LONG,
BROAD, and
SHARPSIGHT

LONG,
BROAD, and
SHARPSIGHT

A Slovak Folktale

Told by I. K. JUNNE
Illustrated by SYLVIE SELIG

Doubleday & Company, Inc., Garden City, New York

Library of Congress Catalog Card Number 76-101432   Text Copyright © 1971 by I. K. Junne
Illustrations Copyright © 1971 by Sylvie Selig   All Rights Reserved. Printed in the United States of America

Long ago in a dim and distant past, magic was king, and every wise man had a trick or two up his sleeve. Three extraordinary men rode together then, far and wide across the land—and made their way serving kings and princes. They were called Long, Broad, and Sharpsight.

Long was tall and thin. He could stretch and stretch and stretch until he stood above the highest forest.

Broad was short and fat. He could make himself wider and wider and wider until he filled a vast plain.

Sharpsight had eyes that could see into the deepest ocean or the darkest forest. He wore a blindfold. For if he gazed sharply at anything, it would burst into flame or shatter into a thousand pieces. Even blindfolded, he could see far across the land.

One day these three comrades were riding in search of a lord to serve. They came upon a sad young prince riding alone in the forest.

"Hail, good prince. What saddens you?" asked the three.

"My true love sits in prison in the iron castle, and a wicked wizard watches over her. I must set her free," the prince answered.

"How did she come to be captured, sire?" asked the three.

"I know not," said the young prince. "I only know I must find her and set her free."

Thereupon, he told the three comrades how he had come to fall in love with the captive princess.

"My father, the king, is growing old and he bade me to choose a wife while he still lives.

"He sent me up to a tower. Nobody within the memory of man had ever been up there or knew what lay hidden there. In the tower were twelve high windows in golden frames, and on each window was a fair damsel, painted with the colors of the rainbow. Each was more lovely than the next.

"The twelfth window was covered with a white curtain. Behind it was the fairest damsel of all, dressed in a white dress trimmed with a silver girdle. On her head was a crown of pearls. Her face was pale and her eyes sad.

"As I gazed upon her, my heart felt a sweet and bitter pain. I vowed then to take her as my bride.

"When I told my father, he was saddened and told me she was kept captive by a wicked wizard. All others who have tried to free her have turned to stone.

"But my father gave me his blessing. 'What's done cannot be undone. The plighted word is law. Go try your luck and return home safely,' he said."

"Be sad no more, good prince," said the three. "We can help you."

"What can you do for me?" asked the prince.

"I can extend myself," said Long, stretching until his head was in the clouds.

"I can widen myself," said Broad, blowing himself out until he pushed the prince and his comrades right out of the forest.

"I can see far and wide and my gaze can split the hardest stone," said Sharpsight and fixed his gaze on a nearby rock until it splintered into a thousand pieces.

"Ride with me then," said the prince. "Not every day will I find such men as you."

Thereupon, Sharpsight looked hither and yon until he spied the iron castle. Then Long extended himself and placed the company at the gate of the castle.

No sooner had they ridden through the gate than it clanged shut, and they were captives in the iron castle.

They put their horses in the stables which had been made ready for them. Then they went into the castle hall. They saw many lords and ladies dressed in fine silks and jewels. But not one of them moved. They had all been turned to stone.

They made their way to the dining hall and found a rich banquet laid out for four and ate and drank their fill.

When they had finished eating, the door flew open, and the wicked wizard stood in their midst. He was a bent old man and wore a long black robe. Though his head was bald, he had a gray beard down to his knees. He wore three iron hoops instead of a girdle. By the hand, he led a beautiful damsel dressed in a white dress trimmed with a silver girdle. On her head she wore a crown of pearls, but she was sad and pale as if she had risen from the grave.

The prince recognized her immediately and his heart pained him. Before he could utter a word, the old wizard spoke.

"I know you have come to take the princess away. It will not be easy. All others who have tried have failed and been turned to stone. Here is what you must do. You must watch over the princess for three nights. If she doesn't vanish from you after the third night, you may take her away. If she vanishes, you and your servants will be turned to stone like all who have come before you."

Then the wicked wizard withdrew and left the princess with them.

She spoke to no one nor did she smile or even turn her head. It was as if she were made of marble.

But the prince could not take his eyes off her. He sat beside her and determined not to sleep all night long lest she should vanish.

Long extended himself like a strap and wound himself around the whole room along the wall.

Broad posted himself in the doorway, swelled himself up, and stopped it up so tight not even a mouse could slip through.

Sharpsight kept watch.

But soon they all began to nod and fall asleep, for the wicked wizard had cast a spell on them. And during the night the princess vanished.

At daybreak the prince woke up and found that the princess was gone. He was so distressed he didn't know which way to turn. He ran about and shook each of his comrades awake.

"The princess is gone! What can we do? What can we do?"

His comrades immediately took the situation in hand. Sharpsight looked sharply out the window.

"I see her already, sire," he said. "A hundred miles hence is a forest, in the midst of the forest an old oak and on top of the oak an acorn. She is that acorn."

Long immediately extended himself and went ten miles at a step, while Sharpsight sat on his shoulders and pointed the way.

The prince paced the floor anxiously even though they were gone but a few minutes. When they returned, Long gave the acorn to the prince and said, "Let it fall on the ground, sire."

When the prince let it fall, the princess appeared beside him.

And when the sun began to show itself beyond the mountains, the wicked wizard strode into the room, smiling gleefully. But when he saw the princess, he frowned and growled. Bang! One of the iron hoops he wore splintered and sprang off him. He took the damsel by the hand and led her away.

The next night the wicked wizard brought the princess back. Once again the prince and his comrades determined to stay awake and watch over her. But it was no use. The wizard had cast his spell, and they were soon fast asleep. Once again the prince woke at dawn and found that the princess had vanished.

He immediately wakened Sharpsight. "The princess is gone! Can you see her?"

Sharpsight got up, rubbed his eyes, and looked sharply out the window.

"I see her, sire. There's a mountain two hundred miles off and in the mountain a rock and in the rock a precious stone, and she's that precious stone."

Once again Long took Sharpsight on his shoulders and went twenty miles at a step. Sharpsight fixed his flaming eyes on the mountain; the mountain crumbled and the rock in it split into a thousand pieces, and amongst them glittered the precious stone.

They carried the precious stone to the prince, and when he let it fall on the ground, the princess again stood there.

The wicked wizard was shocked when he came in and saw her there. His eyes flashed with spite. He growled and stamped his foot. Bang! Another iron hoop splintered and fell. Once again he led the princess away.

After supper, the wicked wizard brought the princess in again. "Tonight we will see who wins," he said.

The prince and his companions paced around the room, trying to stay awake. But it was no use. They were bewitched. Once again they fell asleep, and once again the princess vanished.

When the prince awoke and found her gone again, he immediately woke Sharpsight.

Sharpsight looked out for a long time. "Oh, sire," he said, "the princess is a long way off, a long way off. Three hundred miles hence is a black sea and in the midst of the sea a shell and in the shell a gold ring, and she's the ring. But never fear, we'll fetch her. Today, Broad must come with us; we shall need him."

Long took Sharpsight on one shoulder and Broad on the other and went thirty miles at a step.

When they came to the black sea, Long extended his arm as far as he could, but he could not reach the bottom where the shell was.

Broad stepped forward. "Wait comrades, I can help you." He swelled himself out as far as his paunch would stretch and lay down on the shore and drank and drank. In a very short time, the water fell so low that Long easily reached the bottom and took the shell out of the sea. He extracted the ring from the shell, took his comrades on his shoulders, and hastened back.

He found it difficult to run with Broad who had half a sea of water inside him. So he cast him from his shoulder to the ground in a wide valley.

Whomp! He fell like a sack of water from a tower. In a moment the whole valley was under water like a vast lake. Broad himself barely crawled out of it.

Meanwhile, back at the castle, the prince was in trouble! Dawn was fast approaching. The prince paced back and forth, and perspiration broke out on his forehead.

Soon the sun showed itself in the east like a thin slip of flame. Then with a loud crash the door flew open, and on the threshold stood the wizard. When he saw that the princess was gone, he laughed a hateful laugh and rubbed his hands together. He was about to turn the prince to stone.

Sharpsight saw what danger the prince was in and told Long who hurled the ring through the castle window. When it fell to the floor, the princess again stood in the room.

The wicked wizard roared with rage until the castle quaked.

Bang! The third iron hoop sprang off him. The wizard turned into a raven and flew away through the shattered window.

Then the beautiful damsel spoke. She thanked the prince for setting her free, and blushed like a rose.

Then all the lords and ladies who had been turned to stone came to life again. Joy and merriment filled the castle.

The lords gathered to thank the prince for their freedom.

"Your thanks is not for me but for my comrades," he told them. "Without Long, Broad, and Sharpsight, I too would have been turned to stone. They outwitted the wicked wizard."

The prince started for home with his bride and his comrades. The old king wept for joy at the sight of his son and planned a magnificent wedding for him. The festivities lasted three weeks.

When the wedding festivities ended, Long, Broad, and Sharpsight told the prince they were going into the world again to look for work. The prince begged them to stay and offered to give them anything they desired. But they were restless.

Long, Broad, and Sharpsight bade farewell to the prince and his beautiful bride and rode off in search of adventure.